# Dear Parent:

Congratulations! Your child is taking the first steps on an exciting journey. The destination? Independent reading!

**STEP INTO READING®** will help your child get there. The program offers five steps to reading success. Each step includes fun stories and colorful art. There are also Step into Reading Sticker Books, Step into Reading Math Readers, Step into Reading Write-In Readers, Step into Reading Phonics Readers, and Step into Reading Phonics First Steps! Boxed Sets—a complete literacy program with something for every child.

## Learning to Read, Step by Step!

### Ready to Read   Preschool–Kindergarten
• big type and easy words • rhyme and rhythm • picture clues
For children who know the alphabet and are eager to begin reading.

### Reading with Help   Preschool–Grade 1
• basic vocabulary • short sentences • simple stories
For children who recognize familiar words and sound out new words with help.

### Reading on Your Own   Grades 1–3
• engaging characters • easy-to-follow plots • popular topics
For children who are ready to read on their own.

### Reading Paragraphs   Grades 2–3
• challenging vocabulary • short paragraphs • exciting stories
For newly independent readers who read simple sentences with confidence.

### Ready for Chapters   Grades 2–4
• chapters • longer paragraphs • full-color art
For children who want to take the plunge into chapter books but still like colorful pictures.

**STEP INTO READING®** is designed to give every child a successful reading experience. The grade levels are only guides. Children can progress through the steps at their own speed, developing confidence in their reading, no matter what their grade.

Remember, a lifetime love of reading starts with a single step!

*To Jilly Jake and the*
*original Peanut*
*—H.K.*

Text copyright © 2003 by Heidi Kilgras.
Illustrations copyright © 2003 by Mike Reed.
All rights reserved under International and Pan-American Copyright Conventions.
Published in the United States by Random House Children's Books, a division of
Random House, Inc., New York, and simultaneously in Canada by Random House
of Canada Limited, Toronto.

www.stepintoreading.com

Educators and librarians, for a variety of teaching tools, visit us at
www.randomhouse.com/teachers

*Library of Congress Cataloging-in-Publication Data*
Kilgras, Heidi.
Peanut / by Heidi Kilgras ; illustrated by Mike Reed.
    p.   cm. — (Step into reading. A step 2 book)
SUMMARY: When a toddler wanders off in the grocery store, the family dog uses its excellent
sense of smell to track down the missing child.
ISBN 0-375-80618-0 (trade) — ISBN 0-375-90618-5 (lib. bdg.)
[1. Dogs—Fiction.  2. Missing children—Fiction.]
I. Reed, Mike, 1951– , ill.  II. Title.  III. Series: Step into reading. Step 2 book.
PZ7.K5553Pe 2003  [E]—dc21  2003010282

Printed in the United States of America   First Edition   20  19  18  17  16  15  14  13

STEP INTO READING, RANDOM HOUSE, and the Random House colophon are registered trademarks
of Random House, Inc.

# Peanut

by Heidi Kilgras

illustrated by Mike Reed

Random House 🏠 New York

This is Peanut.

He is tiny,

but he is strong.

He loves to sniff

things—

even stinky things!

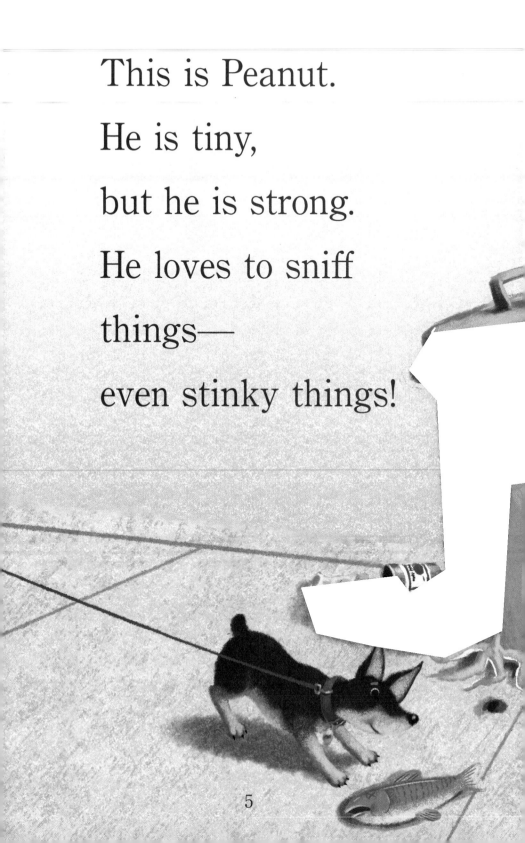

Peanut sniffs a cat.

He sniffs a wad of gum.

He sniffs a trash bag.

"NO, Peanut!" says Nina.
"Stop sniffing everything!"
Peanut sniffs Nina, Tad,
and Mama anyway!

At the store,
Nina puts Peanut
in her backpack.

He can see everything!

Mama pushes the cart.

Nina pushes the stroller.

Tad is asleep.

Nina pretends Peanut
is her baby.

Tad wakes up.
He climbs out
of his stroller.
Off he goes!
Uh-oh!

Nina sees
the empty stroller.
"Where is Tad?" she cries.

Peanut jumps down.

<u>He</u> will find Tad!

"Peanut, come back!"

Nina yells.

Sniff, sniff, sniff.
Peanut's nose is
to the floor.
Is that Tad he smells?

That is not Tad!

Then Peanut hears

a giggle.

Peanut runs
around the corner.
That is not Tad!
But there is a
trail of Tasty O's—
Tad's favorite!

Peanut follows the trail
of Tasty O's.
Munch, munch, munch.
He gobbles them up!

The trail leads
to a dark room.

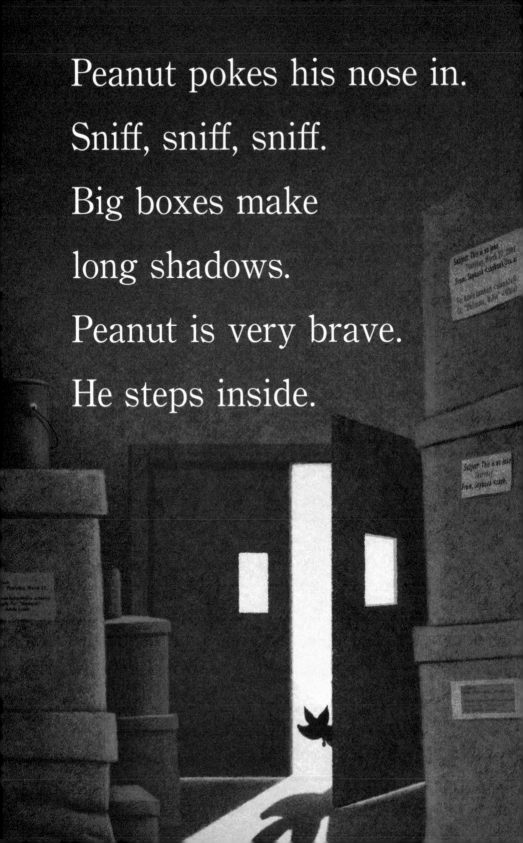

Peanut pokes his nose in.

Sniff, sniff, sniff.

Big boxes make

long shadows.

Peanut is very brave.

He steps inside.

Peanut sniffs again.

He smells food.

He even smells a mouse.

But there is

one more smell . . .

. . . a dirty diaper!

It is Tad!

He is up high.

Peanut has to help him!

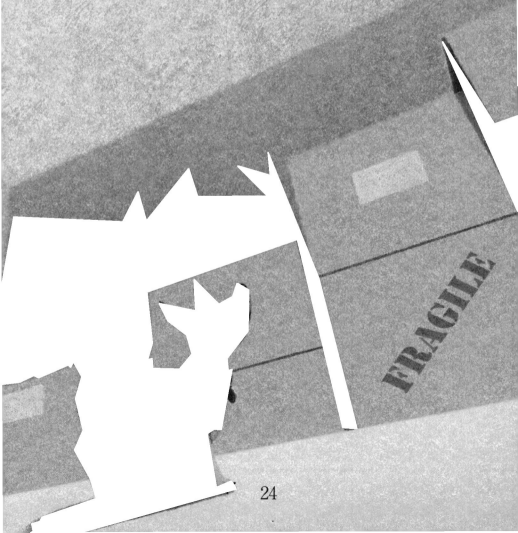

How can Peanut help?

He can bark!

Yip! Yap! WOOF!

Peanut may be tiny,
but he is loud.

Nina and Mama and
the man in the apron
come running.

Mama grabs Tad
and hugs him tight.

Nina scoops Peanut up
in her arms.
He sticks his nose out
and sniffs Tad all over.
He <u>likes</u> stinky things!

"You sure have a
super sniffer, Peanut!"
says Nina.
And Peanut tugs and sniffs
all the way home.